Peggy and the Paper Queen

Om KIDZ
An imprint of Om Books International

Om Kidz | Om Books International

Reprinted in 2023

Corporate & Editorial Office
A-12, Sector 64, Noida 201 301
Uttar Pradesh, India
Phone: +91 120 477 4100
Email: editorial@ombooks.com
Website: www.ombooksinternational.com

ISBN: 978-93-52760-32-9

Printed in India

10 9 8 7 6 5 4 3 2

Sales Office
107, Ansari Road, Darya Ganj
New Delhi 110 002, India
Phone: +91 11 4000 9000
Email: sales@ombooks.com
Website: www.ombooks.com

Peggy and the Paper Queen

Paste your photograph here

My name is

Peggy is **quite** a clever girl.

Her **parents** are very **proud** of her.

Peggy loves to **paint.**

She **paints plants, people, princes** and **princesses** on **paper.**

She then cuts them out of **paper.**

She **pastes** them on her door.

She draws a **pet puppy** that keeps her company. Its name is **Poppy.**

One day, **Peggy paints** a **picture** of a **queen.**

She cuts her out of **paper.**

She is about to **paste**
her on her door.

Peggy hears someone shouting. It is the **paper queen**. "Don't let me out," shouts the **paper queen**. The **queen** jumps out of the **paper.**

She **pushes Peggy. Peggy** falls down. She cries out in **pain.** The **queen** tries to **poke Peggy** with a **pin.**

Poor Peggy's lovely **pink** dress is caught in the pin. The **paper queen** will not be **quiet.**

"Why are you doing this?" **Peggy** asks the **queen.**

'You have taken me out of my **palace,"** says the **paper queen** angrily. "**Put** me back at once." **Peggy** knows what she has to do.

She draws a **palace** with a **pencil** and cuts it out.

The **paper queen pops** back into the **palace.**

Peggy quickly shuts
the **paper** door of
the **paper palace.**

The **paper queen**
is inside and happy.

Peggy feeds the **paper queen paper potatoes** and **paper pastries** on a **paper plate.**

She **plays** with her as well.

When **Peggy** wakes up the next morning. The **paper queen** is inside the **paper palace. Peggy** thinks it is a dream. But the **paper queen** winks at **Peggy** from the **page.**

Know your words

Naming words

princes
princesses
paper
puppy
Poppy
picture
pin
palace
pencil
potatoes
pastries
plate
page
pet
queen
question

Describing words

proud
poor
pink

Doing words

paint
pastes
pushes
poke
put
plays
quiet

Sight Words

pain
quite

Decorate the crown of the queen as you like and colour it.

Circle the words beginning with ‘p’.

paper

dream

wink

pastry

poke

cut

inside

princess

Colour the prince and princess.